Small Camel Follows the Star

Rachel W. N. Brown

Illustrated by *Giuliano Ferri*

Albert Whitman & Company, Morton Grove, Illinois

Library of Congress Cataloging-in-Publication Data

Brown, Rachel W. N.
Small Camel follows the star / written by Rachel W. N. Brown ; illustrated by Giuliano Ferri.
p. cm.
Summary: Small Camel is given the honor of carrying a very important package,
as his master Balthazar, a wise man, goes in search of Baby Jesus.
ISBN 10: 0-8075-7453-8   ISBN 13: 978-0-8075-7453-9 (hardcover)
[1. Camels—Fiction. 2. Jesus Christ—Nativity—Fiction. 3. Christmas—Fiction.]
I. Ferri, Giuliano, ill. II. Title.
PZ7.B816685Sm 2007 [E]—dc22 2007001528

Design by Carol Gildar.

For information about Albert Whitman & Company,
please visit our web site at www.albertwhitman.com.

Dedicated to my children:
Dara Lynn, Kay, and Greg—
you are my favorite cheerleaders. —R. W. N. B.

For my father, the greatest teacher of my life. —G. F.

*S*mall Camel was the newest little camel in Balthazar's corral. His feet were too big for his skinny legs. He had a very small hump. But he had big beautiful eyes and long eyelashes.

"I love you," whispered his mama. "You will grow up to be strong. You will carry heavy loads to faraway places. Balthazar will be proud of you."

Balthazar was a wise and wealthy man. He traveled far with his camels. He watched the stars and wrote on long scrolls. The scrolls were covered with important lines and words.

"What do the lines and words mean?" Small Camel asked.

Mama shook her head. "Balthazar knows," she said.

One evening, as the sun began to set, a bright star appeared on the horizon. Balthazar gathered his servants. "This is the great star I have waited so long to see," he told them. "We must prepare for a journey. Groom the camels. Pack enough food and clothing for many weeks of travel across the desert."

Small Camel watched the servants brush the furry coats of the big camels and put blankets on their backs. The saddle that Balthazar would ride was placed on Mama's hump. Many bundles were tied onto the other camels.

Small Camel knew he was too small to carry so much; he would have to stay home. His stomach ached, and he started to cry. He snuggled close to his mother. "I don't want you to go, Mama," he said, sniffling. "When will you come back?"

Just then Balthazar came out of his house dressed in fine traveling clothes. He carried a small bundle and a rope halter. "These are for you, Small Camel," he said. "I don't want you to miss this important journey. I think you are big enough to carry one special package."

Balthazar put the halter around Small Camel's head. He put a beautiful blanket over his hump. He tied the bundle in place.

Small Camel was so excited he could hardly stand still. Where were they going? What was he carrying?

After sunset, Balthazar and his caravan headed out into the
desert. They would travel at night after the hot sun had gone
down. Balthazar rode high on Mama's hump, and Small Camel
walked close behind.

Ahead, the star shone brightly.

The next morning, Balthazar stopped in a small town where the camels were unloaded. There he met two friends, Melchior and Gaspar. The three men got out their scrolls and huddled together. Small Camel could hear them talking about the beautiful star and something else . . . a baby king!

In the evening, the camels were loaded again. Two more packages—one from Melchior and one from Gaspar—were added to Small Camel's hump. Now he was carrying three special bundles. The load was heavier, but it felt just right. What could be in these bundles? Small Camel wondered.

Night after night, Small Camel and his mother walked and walked. Each morning, as the sun was rising, the travelers set up their tents. Balthazar, Melchior, and Gaspar checked their scrolls and marked where the bright star was. The servants prepared food for the travelers. Fresh water and grass were brought for the camels, and everyone rested.

Camels can walk for a long time, even without water, but Small Camel was very young. They had been traveling for months, and he lost count of the days and nights. "Are we there yet, Mama?" he asked. "My feet hurt. When will we find the baby king?"

"I don't know how long the trip will be," said Mama. "But I know Balthazar will take good care of us. We can always trust him." Small Camel felt a little better, but his feet still hurt and he wanted to be at home, resting on fresh straw in his own corner of the corral.

At last, one day at dawn, the caravan came over a hill. Balthazar stopped. The star was shining directly above a village just ahead. "This is the place," he told the weary group. "This is where we will find the baby king."

"Where is the palace, Mama?" Small Camel asked.

"Balthazar will find it," Mama replied.

Balthazar led the caravan through the streets of the town. They followed the light of the star until they could see it shining over a very small house.

"Oh, Mama, there must be a mistake," said Small Camel. "This is a poor man's house. Surely a king wouldn't live here."

Outside, a carpenter named Joseph worked at his bench. He put down his tools and invited the travelers into the courtyard.

Balthazar gently pulled on Small Camel's halter. "Come with me," he said.

Inside the courtyard sat a young woman
named Mary. In her arms she held a beautiful child—
little Jesus.

Small Camel dropped to his knees as he had been
trained. Balthazar spread the blanket on the ground
and put the bundles on it.

And what was in those bundles? Small Camel had been carrying presents! Presents for Jesus!

Melchior unwrapped a chest filled with shining gold.

Balthazar's gift was a pot of spicy frankincense.

Gaspar set out a tall jar of sweet-smelling myrrh.

Mary bounced the baby on her lap. He smiled when he saw the presents. He giggled and clapped his hands at the little camel kneeling before him.

Small Camel forgot how tired he was. He forgot how much his feet hurt. He forgot the long months walking across the sand. He didn't know why the house was not a palace. He didn't know why the baby wasn't wearing a crown. But Small Camel knew this baby was a king.

At last it was time to go. Everyone, even the camels, gathered around Joseph, Mary, and little Jesus. The baby smiled and cooed; his sweet laughter filled the weary travelers with peace.

"I am proud of you," Balthazar whispered to Small Camel. "You have done a very good job carrying those precious gifts."

Small Camel had never been so happy.

Small Camel grew tall and strong, just as his mother knew he would. He traveled often with Balthazar. Together they visited many wonderful places and had wonderful times. But none of the trips was as special to Small Camel as that first trip across the desert, when he carried the presents for Baby Jesus.